KUBRICK

Also by Michael Herr:

Dispatches

The Big Room
(with Guy Peellaert)

Walter Winchell

KUBRICK
MICHAEL HERR

Grove Press
New York

Published simultaneously in Canada
Printed in the United States of America

FIRST EDITION

Library of Congress Cataloging-in-Publication Data

Herr, Michael, 1940-
  Kubrick / Michael Herr.
    p.   cm.
  ISBN 0-8021-1670-1
    1. Kubrick, Stanley. I. Title.

PN1998.3.K83 H47 2000
791 .43'0233'092—dc21
[B]

00-027678

Design by Laura Hammond Hough

Grove Press
841 Broadway
New York, NY 10003

00 01 02 03 10 9 8 7 6 5 4 3 2 1

Acknowledgments

I want to offer a brief but sincere word of thanks to Graydon Carter and Wayne Lawson of *Vanity Fair*, and to Tony Frewin, Leon Vitali, and Jan Harlan, for their help in the writing of this book.

KUBRICK

1

Somehow or other we get into this rather heavy rap—about death, and infinity, and the origin of time—you know the sort of thing.

—Terry Southern

STANLEY KUBRICK was a friend of mine, insofar as people like Stanley have friends, and as if there *are* any people like Stanley now. Famously reclusive, as I'm sure you've heard, he was in fact a complete failure as a recluse, unless you believe that a recluse is simply someone who seldom leaves his house. Stanley saw a lot of people. Sometimes he even went out to see people, but not often, very rarely, hardly ever. Still, he was one of the most gregarious men I ever knew, and it didn't change anything that most of this conviviality went on over the phone. He viewed the telephone the way

Mao viewed warfare, as the instrument of a protracted offensive where control of the ground was critical and timing crucial, while time itself was meaningless, except as something to be kept on your side. An hour was nothing, mere overture, or opening move, or gambit, a small taste of his virtuosity. The writer Gustav Hasford claimed that he and Stanley were once on the phone for seven hours, and I went over three with him many times. I've been hearing about all the people who say they talked to Stanley on the last day of his life, and however many of them there were, I believe them all.

Somebody who knew him forty-five years ago when he was starting out said, "Stanley always acted like he knew something you didn't know," but honestly, he didn't have to act. Not only that, by the time he was through having what he called, in quite another context, "strenuous intercourse" with you, he knew most of what you knew as well. Hasford called him an earwig; he'd go in one ear and not come out the other until he'd eaten clean through your head.

He had the endearing and certainly seductive habit when he talked to you of slipping your name in every few sentences, particularly in the punch line, and there was always a punch line. He had an especially fraternal temperament anyway, but I know quite a few women who found him extremely charming. A few of them were even actresses.

Some Americans move to London and in three weeks they're talking like Denholm Elliott. Stanley picked up the odd English locution, but it didn't take Henry Higgins to place him as pure, almost stainless Bronx. Stanley's voice was very fluent, melodious even. In spite of the Bronx nasal-caustic, perhaps the shadow of some adenoidal trauma long ago, it was as close to the condition of music as speech can get and still be speech, like a very well-read jazz musician talking, with a pleasing and graceful Groucho-like rushing and ebbing of inflection for emphasis, suggested quotation marks and even inverted commas to convey amused disdain, over-enunciating phrases that struck him as fabulously banal, with lots of *innuendo*, and lots of latent sarcasm, and some not so latent, lively tempi, brilliant timing, eloquent silences; and always, masterful, seamless segues, "Lemme change the subject for just a minute," or, "What were we into before we got into *this*?" I never heard him try to do other voices, or dialects, even when he was telling Jewish jokes. Stanley quoted other people all the time, people in "the industry" whom he'd spoken to that afternoon (Steven and Mike, Warren and Jack, Tom and Nicole), or people who died a thousand years ago, but it was always Stanley speaking.

When I met him in 1980, I was not just a subscriber to the Stanley legend, I was frankly susceptible to it. He'd heard that I was living in London from a mutual friend, David Cornwell (b.k.a. John le Carré), and invited us for dinner and a movie. The movie was a screening of *The Shining* at Shepperton Studios a few weeks before its American release, followed by dinner at Childwick Bury, the 120-acre estate near St. Albans, an hour north of London, that Stanley and his family and their dogs and cats had just moved into. Stanley wanted to meet me because he'd liked my book about Vietnam. It was the first thing he said to me when we met. The second thing he said to me was that he didn't want to make a movie of it. He meant this as a compliment, sort of, but he also wanted to make sure I wasn't getting any ideas. He'd read the book several times looking for the story in it, and quoted bits of it, some of them quite long, from memory during dinner. And since I'd loved his movies for something like twenty-five years by this time, I was touched, flattered, and very happy to meet him, because I was of course fairly aware that it was unusual to meet him. Stanley wasn't someone you ran into at a party and struck up a relationship with.

He was thinking about making a war movie next, but he wasn't sure which war, and in fact, now that he mentioned it, not even so sure he wanted to make a war movie at all.

He called me a couple of nights later to ask me if I'd read any Jung. I had. Was I familiar with the concept of the Shadow, our hidden dark side? I assured him that I was. We did half an hour on the Shadow, and how he really wanted to get it into his war picture. And oh, did I know of any good Vietnam books, "You know, Michael, something with a *story?*" I didn't. I told him that after seven years working on a Vietnam book and nearly two more on *Apocalypse Now*, it was almost the last thing in the world I was interested in. He thanked me for my honesty, my "almost blunt candor," and said that, probably, what he most wanted to make was a film about the Holocaust, but good luck putting all of *that* into a two-hour movie. And then there was this other book he was fascinated by, he was fairly sure I'd never heard of it, Arthur Schnitzler's 1926 novella *Traumnovelle*, which translates as *Dream Novel*, meaninglessly called *Rhapsody* in the only English edition available at that time. He'd read it more than twenty years before, and bought rights to it in the early seventies (it's the book that *Eyes Wide Shut* is based on), and the reason I'd probably never heard of it (he started to laugh) was that he'd bought up every single existing copy of it. Maybe he'd send me one. I could read it and tell him what I thought.

"You know, just read it and we'll talk, I'm interested to know what you think. And Michael, ask around among your friends from the war, maybe *they* know a good Vietnam story. You know, like at the next American Legion meeting? Oh, and Michael. . . . Do me a favor will you?"

"Sure."

"Don't tell anybody what we've been talking about . . ."

The next afternoon, a copy of the Schnitzler book arrived, along with the paperback edition of Raul Hilberg's enormous *The Destruction of the European Jews*, delivered by Stanley's driver, Emilio, who whether I realized it or not was about to become my new best friend.

I read the Schnitzler right away, and that's when I had my early inkling of how smart Stanley really was. *Traumnovelle*, published in Vienna in 1926, is the full, excruciating flowering of a voluptuous and self-consciously decadent time and place, a shocking and dangerous story about sex and sexual obsession and the suffering of sex. In its pitiless view of love, marriage, and desire, made all the more disturbing by the suggestion that either all of it, or maybe some of it, or possibly none of it is a dream, it intrudes on the concealed roots of Western erotic life like a laser, suggesting discreetly, from behind its dream cover, things that are seldom even privately acknowledged, and *never* spoken of in daylight. Stanley thought it would be perfect for Steve Martin. He'd loved *The Jerk*.

He'd talked about this book with a lot of people, David Cornwell and Diane Johnson among them, and since David and Diane and I later talked about it among ourselves (and out of Stanley's hearing, I think), I know that his idea for it in those days was always as a sex comedy, but with a wild and somber streak running through it. This didn't make a lot of sense to us, we were just responding to the text as a work of literary art, and not a very funny one. Maybe *Traumnovelle* is a comedy in the sense that *Don Giovanni* is: attempted rape and compulsive pathetic list-keeping, implied impotence and the Don dragged down into hell forever, the old sex machine ignorant and defiant to the end. A pretty severe and upsetting comedy, not very *giocoso*, and not the essence of *Traumnovelle*, which more than anything else was sinister. The way we writers saw it, it was as frightening as *The Shining*. Now I think we were all too square to imagine what Stanley saw in Steve Martin, because this was not *The Jerk*. This could have turned out to be another one of those stories you heard so many times about him, usually from cameramen and other high-echelon crew, *Stanley said we should try to do it this way and I said it's never been done this way, and it can't be done this way, the wrong stops on the wrong lens on the wrong camera, and he did it anyway, and he was right.*

We talked about it for years, starting that afternoon, because I don't think Emilio could have made it back to St. Albans before Stanley called, "Didja read it? What do you think?" After about an hour, he asked if I'd had a chance to look at the Hilberg book yet. I reminded him that I'd only just gotten it.

When he sent you a book, he wanted you to read it, and not just read it, but to drop everything and get *into* it. John Calley, who was probably Stanley's closest friend, told me that when he was head of production at Warner Bros. in the seventies and first working with him, Stanley sent him a set of *The Golden Bough*, unabridged, and then bugged him every couple of weeks for a year about reading it.

Finally, Calley said, "Stanley, I've got a studio to run. I don't have time to read mythology." "It isn't mythology, John," Stanley said. "It's your *life*."

I picked up the Hilberg many times and laid it down again. I finally read it only a few years ago, when I knew there was no possibility that Stanley would ever use it for a film, and I could see why Stanley was so absorbed by it. It was a forbidding volume, densely laid out in a two-column format, nearly eight hundred pages long, small print, heavily footnoted, so minutely detailed that one would have to be more committed than I was at the moment to its inconceivably dreadful subject. I could see that it was exhaustive; it certainly *looked* like hard work, and it read like a complete log of the Final Solution. And every couple of weeks, Stanley would call and ask me if I'd read it yet, "You should read it, Michael, it's *monumental*!" This went on for months.

Finally I said, "Stanley, I can't make it."

"Why not?"

"I don't know. I guess right now I just don't want to read a book called *The Destruction of the European Jews*."

"No, Michael," he said. "The book you don't want to read right now is *The Destruction of the European Jews*, Part Two."

"You know, Michael, it's not absolutely true in every case that nobody likes a smart-ass," Stanley was saying.

I once described 1980–83 as a single phone call lasting three years, with interruptions. This serial call had many of the characteristics of the college bull session, long free-form late-night intellectual inquiries, discursions, conversations, displays, like talking to a very smart kid in a dorm room until three in the morning, and I'd think, *Doesn't this guy get tired?* But then Stanley never went to college; he was only a stunningly accomplished autodidact, one of those people we may hear about but rarely meet, the almost but not quite legendary Man On Whom Nothing Is Lost.

"Hey Michael, didja ever read *Herodotus*? The Father of *Lies?*" or, "Frankly, I've never understood why Schopenhauer is considered so pessimistic. *I* never thought he was pessimistic, did *you*, Michael?," laughing at the four or five things he found so funny in this, with a winsome touch of self-deprecation, half-apologetic. *It's not* my *fault I'm so smart.* And I'd think, *Doesn't he have anything else to* do? But this *is* what he did. These calls were about information. They were about Stanley's work.

We'd be talking about something, like why "most war movies always look so phony," or why we thought this movie or that book was such a hit, and we'd be suddenly off across two thousand years of Western culture, "from Plato to NATO." He was just an old-fashioned social Darwinist (seemingly), with layer upon layer of the old, now vanishing, liberal humanism, disappointed but undimmed, and without contradiction; if he made no distinctions between Art and Commerce, or Poetry and Technology, or even Personal and Professional, why should he make them between "Politics" and Philosophy?

Stanley had views on everything, but I wouldn't exactly call them political. ("Hey Michael, what's the definition of a neoconservative?. . . A liberal who's just been *mugged*, ha ha ha ha.") His views on democracy were those of most people I know, neither left nor right, not exactly brimming with belief, a noble failed experiment along our evolutionary way, brought low by base instincts, money and self-interest and stupidity. (If a novelist expresses this view he's a visionary, seemingly, but if a movie director does, he's a misanthrope.) He thought the best system might be under a benign despot, although he had little belief that such a man could be found. He wasn't exactly a cynic, but he could easily have passed for one. He was certainly a capitalist. He believed himself to be a realist. He was known to be a tough guy. The way I see him, essentially, he was an artist to his fingertips, and he needed a lot of cover, and a lot of control.

For the most part we talked about writers, usually dead and white and Euro-American, hardly the current curriculum: Stendhal (half an hour), Balzac (two hours), Conrad, Crane, Hemingway (hours and hours—"Do you think it was true that he was drunk all the time, even when he wrote? Yeah? Well, I'll have to find out what he was drinking and send a case to all my writers."), Céline ("My favorite anti-Semite."), and Kafka, who he thought was the greatest writer of the century, and the most misread: People who used the word "Kafkaesque" had probably never read Kafka. I'd read *The Golden Bough*, and didn't have to go through that again, but he urged me to check out Machiavelli, and *The Art of War* (years before Michael Ovitz slipped him a copy), and Veblen's *The Theory of the Leisure Class*. He had a taste and a gift for the creative-subversive, and he dug Swift and Malaparte and William Burroughs, and was interested to know that Burroughs was a friend of mine. I got him to read Faulkner, *Absalom, Absalom!;* he thought it was incredibly beautiful, but "there's no movie in it. I mean, where's the *weenie*, Michael?" Then he'd be into something else, the "inevitable" fiscal and social disaster lurking in the burgeoning mutual funds market, or how he'd like to make a movie about doctors because "everybody hates doctors" (his father was a doctor), or the savage abiding mystery of Mother Russia, or why opera was "quite possibly the greatest art form" except, oh yeah, maybe for the movies. Then he'd dish about the movies.

"Always thinking, huh Stanley?" I said after one of those exhausting (for me) rooftop-to-rooftop riffs of his. I felt that these calls were starting to take up most of my time, yet I knew they didn't take up most of his, that he was doing other things, "many many of them." I acquired a sense of awe at the energy that had coincided so forcefully with my own. You really needed your chops for this, you'd feel like some poor traveler caught in a ground blizzard, three to thirty times a week and mostly after ten at night, when he usually started wailing. Sometimes, I'd duck his calls.

We talked this way, with occasional visits to the house, dinners and movies, until he found Gustav Hasford's *The Short-Timers*, bought the rights, wrote a long treatment of it, and asked me to work on the script with him. Then we really started talking. By then I knew I'd been working for Stanley from the minute I met him.

Stanley could never be accused of breaking any sumptuary laws. He may have been the master of Childwick Bury, but he dressed like a cottager, and it was very becoming, too. He wore the same thing every day, beat chinos, some sort of work shirt, usually in one of the darker shades of blue, a ripstop cotton fatigue jacket with many pockets, a pair of running shoes, so well broken-in that you almost might think he was a runner (and not a man who liked to be seated), and an all-weather anorak. He had something like a dozen or so sets of this outfit in his closet, so he changed his clothes every day but never his wardrobe. When his daughter Katharina got married in 1984, he went to the Marks and Spencer in St. Albans and bought a dark blue suit for eighty-five quid, a white shirt and a tie, and a pair of black shoes from one of the High Street shoe shops that he told me were made of cardboard. But he had never been admired for his dress sense. Even back in the late fifties, when he was working in Hollywood, the insouciance of his attire was remarked upon by many producers and actors, who thought that he dressed like a beatnik.

Body-blocked, and uncomfortable in physical contact, even his handshake was a bit awkward. The last time I saw him—we hadn't seen each other in four years—he actually put an arm around my shoulder, but I think he felt he might have gone too far, and quickly withdrew it. I don't mean to suggest that Stanley was not a warm person, only that he didn't express it in kissing or hugging or even touching, except with his animals. Apollonian not Dionysian, I couldn't see him on the dance floor breaking hearts. He hated being photographed, and the few glimpses of Stanley on film, in his daughter Vivian Kubrick's documentary *The Making of The Shining*, show a man who clearly doesn't want to be there at all. He never had the impulse to slip around to the other side of the camera like Orson Welles or John Huston or Alfred Hitchcock. I think he felt that he impressed quite enough of himself on his films without that.

He'd once been a chain smoker, and would mooch the odd cigarette, but very rarely. He wasn't especially appetitive, except where information was concerned. He ate temperately, almost never took a drink, and was drug-free. Stanley had a lot of self-control, to put it mildly a hundredfold.

He had small fine hands that he rarely used when he talked, with slender white fingers, expressive even in repose, although they were often in his beard, or up to his glasses for a compulsive adjustment. He had an odd habitual gesture, a stiff sweeping movement of the arm, indicating some low-rent real estate of the mind, "Over there, where we don't want to be." He had small feet, rather dainty, and they moved him along very quickly and smoothly. When I saw him on a set after years of only seeing him in his house, I was amazed at how fast he moved, and how light, darting around the crew and cameras like one of the Sugar Rays, grace and purpose in motion.

Totally contained physically, everything else about him, all the action going on behind the forehead, was in constant play, and it showed—black beard and black hair horseshoeing back now from his high brow to the crown of his head; he looked like he took care of his teeth; and although his mouth wasn't particularly sensual, he had an interesting repertoire of smiles, expressing a wide range of thought and irony and amusement.

As for his famous eyes, described as dark, focused, and piercing, he looked out from a perceptibly deep place, and the look went far inside of you, if you were what he happened to be looking at. Only extremely startled people ever get their eyes open that wide. I know that quite a few people, mostly actors, have unraveled when they got caught in Stanley's beams, even though there was rarely much anger in them. Stanley's look was just so *deliberate*, cool as functioning intelligence itself, demanding satisfaction, or resolution, some kind of answer to some kind of problem before the next problem arose, which it would. Life was problem-solving, and to solve a problem you have to *see* the problem. The eyebrows, especially when arched, were the coup de grâce.

After I moved back to America in 1991, the calls fell off a bit to something like once a month. Usually he'd open with, "Now Michael, don't ask me anything about what I'm doing, okay?" I knew, but not from him, that he'd optioned the rights to a book I'd had sent to him in bound galleys, a possible way to make a two-hour Holocaust film, Louis Begley's *Wartime Lies*, which Stanley adapted and called *Aryan Papers*; I heard he'd talked to Julia Roberts and Uma Thurman about it. He'd also been working with Brian Aldiss and a couple of other writers on *AI*, a cyber-age version of "the Pinocchio myth," which he scrapped because he thought it would be too expensive to make, until he saw *Jurassic Park* and started calling Steven Spielberg every twenty minutes to talk about the technology he'd used. I heard about Tom Cruise and Nicole Kidman and *Eyes Wide Shut*. Then, sometime in 1996, he called.

"Hey Michael, what do you charge these days for a wash and a rinse?"

He was four or five months away from shooting *Eyes Wide Shut*, with a script he'd written with Frederic Raphael.

The story was set in New York in the nineties, and he felt it needed "a little colloquializing."

"You know, like, when someone says 'Hello' it should read 'Hi.' (Laughing.) It needs your *ear*, Michael. It's perfect for you."

"How long?"

"At the very most, two weeks. But it isn't about *how long*. It's about the *magic* . . ." He was laughing, but he meant it.

Of course, he wouldn't send the script he wanted "colloquialized" to me to read. I'd have to go to England and read it in his house, and once you walked in that door, it wasn't always so easy to walk out again. I didn't want to leave my family or my work and get into that kind of involvement with him again without some assurances. I said I'd only do it as a member of the Writers' Guild, and that he'd definitely have to talk to my agent, Sam Cohn, at ICM. I told him that Sam was extremely intelligent and discreet, and besides, this was a Tom Cruise movie, and I felt that agents were appropriate, even required. I knew he'd never call Sam, and he never did. He wanted this to be between us, for a complex of reasons involving money and secrecy, affection and control, respect and pathology and old times' sake. Stanley tried over the next few weeks to get me to change my mind, just drop everything and come over, but I couldn't. When I think of all the ways he had of getting people to do what he wanted them to do, and of how much I liked him, I surprised myself.

"Come on Michael," he said, "it'll be fun."

And that was the problem. If you had anything even resembling a life, time and money and Stanley's will could be a deadly infusion. I think I hurt his feelings. Over the next two and a half years, as I read about the ever-expanding shooting schedule, I pictured myself chained to a table in his house, endlessly washing and rinsing for laughs and minimum wage, strenuous unprotected intercourse, and I had no regrets. Now, of course, I have a few.

I can hear my previous agent now all the way from 1983, when he'd just received Stanley's offer for my writing services on *Full Metal Jacket.* Rendered almost inarticulate by representational indignation, he taunted, "Little Stanley Kubrick wants his *bar mitzvah money*" (a Jewish man talking to a Jewish man about another Jewish man), adding, "And *it isn't even his money!*," obviously impressed, as we all were, by the nerve of the guy.

Stanley was a good friend, and wonderful to work with, but he was a terrible man to do business with, *terrible.* His cheapness was proverbial, and it's true that in the matter of deal-making, whether it was his money or Warner Bros.' money, it flowed down slow and thin, and sometimes not at all, unless you were a necessary star, and even then it bugged him for years that Jack Nicholson made more money from *The Shining* than he did. If, I feel I should add, Nicholson really did.

Stanley's money pathology was one of the most amazing behavioral phenomenons I've ever witnessed. In spite of the care he took, and the tremendous price he paid, to distance himself in all ways from the brutal greedy men who ran Hollywood, a piece of him was always heart to heart with them, elective affinity, and he would sometimes use their methods. It's possible that a few of Stanley's ships sailed under Liberian registration, that his word was not necessarily his bond; and it's true, if you were only in for the money, I can see where you would feel undercompensated, some have said ripped off.

Stanley was The Big Fisherman. He played everybody like a fish, but all different fish, from the majestic salmon to the great white shark, from the agile trout to the sluggish mudfish, each to be played in its particular way according to the speed of the current and the fighting capacity of his adversary, and, of course, his desire and even need for the fish. Sometimes there was just more fight than play, and he'd cut bait, but much more often there were the ones who couldn't wait to jump right into his boat and knock themselves out, because after all he was Stanley Kubrick.

And he knew it, had every reason to know it. It really was Stanley's feeling that it was a privilege to be working with him, and it wasn't remotely the way it sounds, it was a reality that existed far beyond any question of arrogance or humility. I agreed with it then, and nothing ever happened to make me feel any different. Still, it made him happy, knowing that I would never make more than the lamest pro forma difficulties over what he loved to call "emoluments." Probably somewhere he pitied me for being so careless with my "price," for offering him my soft white throat like that, knowing as I did that he would never find it on his pathological screen not to take advantage of it.

"Gee, Michael, you're such a pure guy," almost drooling with sarcasm.

"Are you calling me a schmuck, Stanley?" And my agent's words would pop into my head.

Stanley hadn't really been bar mitzvahed. He was barely making it in school; he couldn't do junior high English, let alone Hebrew, and besides, Dr. and Mrs. Kubrick weren't very religious, and anyway, Stanley didn't want to. He was not what anybody would have called well rounded. From the day he entered grade school in 1934, his attendance record had been a mysterious tissue of serial and sustained absences, his discipline nonexistent or at least nonapparent, his grades shocking. He'd received Unsatisfactory on Works and Plays Well with Others, Respects Rights of Others, and, inevitably, Personality. He did all right in physics, but he graduated high school with a 70 average, and college was out of the question. At seventeen he was already working as a freelance photographer for *Look* magazine, and he joined the staff, and he played a lot of chess, and read a lot of books, and otherwise arranged for his own higher education, like all smart people do.

Stanley always seemed supernaturally youthful to his friends. His voice didn't age over the almost twenty years that I knew him. He had a disarming way of "leavening" serious discourse with low adolescent humor, smutty actually, sophomoric, by which I mean a sophomore in high school. (Think of *Lolita*, with its cherry pie, cavity-filling, and limp-noodle jokes, so blatantly smutty, without shame, subversive, which was the idea. He'd set the lyrical-erotic Nabokovian tone and captured an essence of the novel in the opening credit sequence, the tender and meticulous painting of Lolita's toes, and then begun the comedy. What a fabulous shiny moral barometer that movie looked like in 1962 when it was new, and how we loved which way we thought the wind was going to blow.) Everybody brings his adolescence forward through life with him, but Stanley's adolescence was like a spring, not necessarily rising pure, but always fresh, and refreshing, and touching, because you'd get a glimpse at times of someone like Little Stanley in there, an awesomely intelligent teenager in a lot of pain keeping his courage up. Sometimes I imagined that I could see his actual adolescence in all its devious complexity.

In Vincent LoBrutto's biography, *Stanley Kubrick*, there's a photograph of this socially challenged, academically reviled phenom, taken when he was twelve or thirteen, around the time he would have been bar mitzvahed, *if* he'd been bar mitzvahed, like a normal person. As a piece of evidence in some kind of *Citizen Kane* scavenger hunt to establish the character of a legend, it's persuasive in suggesting how this possibly dweeb-like little Jewish kid from the Bronx came to identify so intimately yet so appropriately with Napoleon.

It's as striking and unsettling as photographs he used later in his movies: the late Mr. Haze, "the soul of integrity," whose mean, calculating eyes look down from his widow's bedroom wall (his ashes are displayed in an urn on the bureau), upon the sexual trainwreck-waiting-to-happen, or Jack Torrance, who has "always been at The Overlook," smiling like one possessed in a picture on the hotel wall taken a generation before he was born. Only just pubescent and already temperamentally if not yet *tactically* beyond the possibility of compromise; secretive but frank, focused, willful, serious and seriously amused, not looking at you so much as past you, at what I'd be reluctant to say. I would call it a picture of a very powerful boy, a handful (as I'm sure someone in the house must have called him at least once), maybe not certain of what he wants but unusually clear about what he doesn't want, and won't stand still for; very refined features, delicate but tough, Stanley on the trembling lip of manhood, a preteen face enveloping an ancient soul, like he's already seen them come and seen them go, and so what?

(This photograph could also suggest why, when he came to make his "youth movie," actual youth was completely absent from it. *A Clockwork Orange* was released to unprecedented controversy, odium even, revealing presumptions in the critical "community" about the high order of our so-called civilization that Stanley was affronting here, a condemnation of the ambiguity that has always been the sign of the first-rate. I think he scared himself with that one, which speaks well for any artist; art and life riding so close together and out of control here that there was no time for one to imitate the other, it was pouring from the same fount. The copycat beatings and killings started as soon it was shown in England, and he permanently withdrew it from release there. Right-minded people couldn't believe that he was aware of what a repellent film he'd made, because if he'd been aware he could never have made it. But of course he was aware, and perfectly sincere; he didn't care that it was repellent—it was meant to be repellent—as long as it was beautiful.)

He disliked the usual references to his having been a "chess hustler" in his Greenwich Village days, as though this impugned the gravity and beauty of the exercise, the suggestion that his game wasn't *pour le sport*, or, more correctly, *pour l'art*. To win the game was important of course, to win the money was irresistible, but it was nothing compared to his game, to the searching, endless action of working on his game. But *of course* he was hustling, he was always hustling; as he grew older and moved beyond still photography, chess became movies, and movies became chess by other means. I doubt that he ever thought of chess as just a game, or even as a game at all. I *do* imagine that a lot of people sitting across the board from him got melted, fried, and fragmented, when Stanley let that cool ray come streaming down out of his eyes—talk about penetrating looks and piercing intelligence; here they'd sat down to a nice game of chess, and all of a sudden he was doing the thinking for both of them.

His high school friend the director Alexander Singer went with Stanley to see Eisenstein's *Alexander Nevsky* around this time. "And we hear Prokofiev's score for the battle on the ice, and Stanley never got over that. He bought a record of it and . . . played it over and over and over again," until his kid sister couldn't stand it anymore and broke it. "I think the word 'obsessive' is not unfair."

It's only fair as far as it goes; just as he was multidisciplined, he was variously obsessive, and not fastidious about picking up information, and not afraid of whatever the information might be. Nobody who really thinks he's smarter than everyone else could ask as many questions as he always did. He was beating the *patzers* in the park, working for *Look* magazine, sometimes using a series of still photos to tell stories, sometimes taking pictures of people like Dwight Eisenhower and George Grosz, Montgomery Clift, Frank Sinatra and Joe DiMaggio (and, I'm sure, keeping his eyes and ears open), reading ten or twenty books a week, and trying to see every movie ever made. There was definitely such a thing as a bad movie, but there was no movie not worth seeing. As a kid he'd been part of the neighborhood multitude that poured ritually, communally, in and out of Loew's Paradise and the RKO Fordham two or three times a week, and now he haunted the Museum of Modern Art and the few foreign-film revival houses, the very underground Cinema 16 and the triple-feature houses along 42nd Street.

Reportedly he was already careless, even reckless, in his appearance, mixing his plaids in wild shirt, jacket, and necktie combinations never seen on the street before, disreputable trousers, way-out accidental hairdos. He started infiltrating whatever film facilities were available in the city in those days, hanging around cutting rooms, labs, equipment stores, asking questions, *How do you do that?* and *What would happen if you did this instead?* and *How much do you think it would cost if . . .* He was jazz mad, and went to the clubs, and a Yankees fan, so he went to the ball games too, all of this in New York in the late forties and early fifties, a smart spacey wide-awake kid like that, it's no wonder he was such a hipster, a '40s-bred, '50s-minted, tough-minded, existential, highly evolved classic hipster. His view and his temperament were much closer to Lenny Bruce's than to any other director's, and this was not merely an aspect of his. He had lots of modes and aspects, but Stanley was a hipster all the time.

Just look at the credits of *Killer's Kiss* to see what the twenty-seven-year-old director thought of himself even then. Story

By (no screenplay credit is given), Produced By, and Edited
Photographed and Directed By Stanley Kubrick. But get a
load of the film, too. He made it under severe time and
money limitations, which he addressed like a soldier; and
not a boy soldier either, making virtues out of limitations,
so that even though it's only sixty-seven minutes long it's
not really a small movie. You can see in ten seconds how
infatuated he was with the medium, and how incredibly
adept, every scene packed with ideas, ambition, and already
the mix of clinical exactness and abiding irreality that was
his signature; with appreciation, *hommage*, even the odd
tributary theft (what he started calling "souveniring" later,
when he began picking up on the Vietnam grunt vernacu-
lar), mostly from the Europeans who had given him so much
pleasure and inspiration: Fritz Lang, G. W. Pabst, Vsevelod
Pudovkin, Jean Renoir, Vittorio De Sica, and, always, Max
Ophuls, with that fluent, rapturous, delirious camera of his.
It also has a strange ending, a painful travesty of a happy
ending, where the couple go off together even though we've
seen them both cravenly betray and desert each other to save
their own lives. It's the kind of touch that would come to be
called Kubrickian.

2

Money well timed and properly applied can accomplish anything.

—Thackeray and/or Kubrick, *Barry Lyndon*

WE WERE DRIVING TOWARD BECKTON, an abandoned gasworks in far East London, near the London Docks. It was a late masterpiece of the nineteenth-century Imperial Industrial Style, and Stanley had arranged to blow it up, let the pieces fall exactly where he wanted them to fall, even if it meant countermanding the laws of physics, and re-create Hue, which it already uncannily resembled, built around the same time as the industrial district of the Vietnamese city, and out of the same grand, doomed cultural assumptions. (He never got the thin light of the Southeast England skies to match the opulent light over Vietnam, but whatever could be dressed was dressed à la Kubrick, Stanley studying photographs of palm trees that he'd had taken in Spain, individually choosing from the thousands of trees which ones he wanted in his movie. Very meticulous guy, Stanley.)

Beckton (or Bec Phu, as it was called after its Vietnamization) was around forty miles from his house. He drove us, and he drove the white Porsche that he supposedly only used to tool around his driveway in. He handled the stick with great proficiency. He drove at speeds above sixty, and neither of us wore crash helmets. It may be true, as had been reported so many times, and is in all the books about him, that he wouldn't let anybody driving him go above thirty-five, and would not get in a car without a helmet. It's not unbelievable. His whole hard drive was up there, it would only be prudent to protect it, to say the least. Maybe by the time I knew him, he'd grown reckless.

As we approached the gasworks, Stanley pointed to a row of small, grimy houses across the road from the plant.

"I'll bet they were owned by the company," he said. "They'd rent them out to their laborers and their families. They had them coming and going. It reminds me of the old studio system."

I looked over at them. They were so marginal, so dark.

"I wonder who lives in them now."

"Poor people," Stanley said.

* * *

Stanley liked to quote the songwriter Sammy Cahn, who was asked in an interview which came first, the words or the music. "The check," Sammy said. (Stanley called him "Sammy." He never met him, but they were in the same business.)

He'd say that when he was younger and people used to ask him why he became a movie director, he'd tell them, Because the pay was good. He was excited by the roar of the propellers as big money took off and went flying through the system, circulating and separating into fewer and larger pockets, even if those pockets were not always his own; he just liked knowing that it was going on out there. He had great respect for the box office, if not the greatest respect, and found something to admire in even the most vile movie once it passed a hundred million. For him, that kind of success always produced some kind of wonderful/horrible aura, vox populi, a reflection of a meaningful fragment of the culture that he contemplated so ardently. Stanley never was one of those middle-class American Jewish men who are afraid of success.

He loved the biz, the Industry, the action he observed day and night from his bridge; all those actors and directors and projects, all the dumb energy endlessly turning over in the studios and the P.R. that came with each new product; he loved being a part of it from his amazing remove, and in terms of being a player he didn't see himself as better or worse, higher or lower, than any of them, all of them in play together, playing toward commerce and art, big expensive art and works of art for the cash register, or as I've sometimes thought in his case, art films with blockbuster pretensions.

He wasn't exactly Show People, but he knew a lot about the procedures and protocols: If I mentioned some moment I'd liked in one of his films, he'd say "Showmanship, Michael," with more irony and levels of irony than you can imagine, with so much amusement, and affection, and respect. And modesty.

I'm not claiming that Stanley wasn't self-absorbed, but I don't think that just because he was obsessive-retentive he was a monomaniac, or even any more egocentric than anybody else in the movies. And I suppose that he was selfish, which doesn't exactly make him a freak in the Directors' Guild (or the Writers' Guild either), nor was his particular selfishness uncharacteristic of artists in general, especially when they've acquired the reputation for genius. A powerful vision can be very fragile while it's still only in the mind, and people have gone to extraordinary lengths to protect it. He didn't think he was the only person in the world, or the only director, or even the only great director. I just think that he thought he was the greatest director, although he never said so in so many words.

3

Just because you like my work doesn't mean that I owe you anything.

—Bob Dylan

IT's BEEN SAID by critics that he was misogynistic, although he photographed some women beautifully: Jean Simmons, Susanne Christiane, Sue Lyon, Marisa Berenson, and Nicole Kidman. There are some wonderful women in Stanley's movies, and some of them he had enough respect for that he made them as dangerous as any of the men. And they say he couldn't make love stories, when what they mean is he couldn't make happy love stories, since there's the famously difficult Humbert and Lo, and Redmond Barry's young love for his cousin Nora in *Barry Lyndon.* She marries a pompous cowardly ugly Englishman for her convenience and the convenience of her family, turning Redmond into a fatally hard case. His movies were certainly unromantic, possibly even anti-romantic.

I know from dozens of articles and a few too many books that Stanley was considered to be cold, although this would have to be among people who never knew him. This perception devolved into cant among a lot of critics, who called his work sterile, particularly in the New York circle (what an awful time liberals have had with his movies; what convolutions of reason and belief, what sad denials of pleasure), including some of the best, even Anthony Lane of *The New Yorker*. Writing about *Killer's Kiss*, he says, "Because Kubrick was still learning, and was hobbled by a tight budget, he couldn't help stumbling up against life; the story of his subsequent career has been the slow and maniacal banishment of that young man's riskiness, to the point where feeling, like rainfall, can be measured by the inch." So how many inches for Charlotte Haze's hunger and confusion, or for Humbert's unending torture? How many for the loneliness verging on desperation of a space that's empty beyond conception, and even emptier for the presence of a few humans? How many for Lady Lyndon's humiliation and despair, and for all of Barry's disappointments, however well earned, or for the grief they attempt to share at the death of their child? What about the living hell of Jack Torrance's madness/possession, or the truly unbearable suffering of Marine recruit Pvt. Pyle in *Full Metal Jacket*. Not even Bergman or Bresson showed more suffering in their films. Merciless is not the same as pitiless. In *2001*, even the last words of a dying, sexually ambivalent computer are pitiful. Worse, to some unforgivable, even vicious, violent Droogie Alex, denatured and cast out by Em and Pee and the unspeakable Joe the Lodger, breaks your heart as he walks along the river clutching his life in a parcel, and it's not a comfortable feeling. As Stanley said when we started to write *Full Metal Jacket*, "Well, Michael, it looks like I'm making another Who Do You Root For movie."

Just as it made Stanley happy to know that all was well in the Emolumental Universe, so it upset and offended him to hear stories of profligacy among members of the Industry. This wasn't simply a phobic reaction to waste and folly, it was a response to energy and intelligence that weren't burning like his own, furious and clean. I told him about a dinner I'd had a few nights before with a director, a man whose history had set new industry standards for wretched excess, and there he was again, committing further hubris in a London restaurant, leaving three hundred pounds' worth of wine that had been ordered and opened sitting untouched on the table when we left. Stanley shook his head sadly.

"You see, Michael. These guys don't know how to live like monks."

Michael Herr

I have to apologize for repeating a story I've told before, because I don't know how to describe Stanley to you without it. I'd already begun to think of him that way before he said it, half joking and perfectly serious. His distance from people, his "impersonality," were always attributed to his supposed neuroses, his "misanthropy," but I think they were more probably signs of his clarity. He lived a simple (outer) life, and a largely devotional one, although admittedly secular. His enormous house was as much a studio as a home, a double studio actually, one for him and his movies and one for his wife, Christiane, and her painting. It was a space of perpetual creative activity. He was thought by the press, and so by the public, to be sequestered there, lurking, scheming, like he was Howard Hughes or Dr. Mabuse or the Wizard of Oz, depending on which paper you read. This is because none of them could ever imagine living the kind of life Stanley lived. Anyway, he wasn't misanthropic, he was irreverent; and come to think of it, he wasn't irreverent either.

They say he had no personal life, but that's ridiculous. It would be more correct to say that he had no professional life, since everything he did was personally done, every move and every call he made, every impulse he expressed, was utterly personal, devoted to the making of his movies, which were all personal. In terms of worldly activity, since you'd have to look to the spiritual sector to find anything like it, I never knew anyone who cared so much and so completely about his work.

When we first met I told him secondhand stories about the filming of *Apocalypse Now*, and what a tough shoot it was. "They're all tough, Michael," he said, and they were, at least the way he did it. Yet something (we know it wasn't money) drew people to it, and kept them at it, even into the part of the process where you felt like you were a slave, to it and to him, like he and his movie were inseparable, insatiable, you were trapped in it, even though the door was always open and you were technically, if not always contractually, free to walk through it any time. People stayed, holding on to whatever piece of the prevailing obsession was going around at the moment, dragging massive blocks nights and weekends and holidays in order to build another one of Stanley's pyramids, and whether cheerful or resentful didn't matter that much to him, although he preferred cheerful.

The more highly paid you were, or the closer to the actual shooting, the more enslaved you were likely to be. If you were right there on the set with film running, the pressure could be amazing, or so I was convincingly told by many of the cast and crew of *Full Metal Jacket*. I wasn't the cameraman, or the art director or even a grip, nor, thank God, an actor. I was only on the location two or three times, so maybe I wasn't even properly enslaved at all. I may have rewritten a few scenes twenty or thirty times, I would have done that anyway, but I never had to go through the number of takes Stanley would require. It was everything anyone ever said it was and more, and worse, whatever it took to "get it right," as he always called it. What he meant by that I couldn't say, nor could hundreds of people who have worked for him, but none of us doubted that *he* knew what he meant.

After seeing *Paths of Glory* I remember walking out on the street and thinking that I'd never seen anybody shot and killed in a movie before. I was seventeen, I'd seen a few (thousand) movies, and I soon realized that I'd been seeing it all my life: cowboys shooting Indians, Indians shooting cavalry, cops shooting robbers, good guys shooting bad guys, weak guys shooting strong guys, Japanese and Germans and Americans shooting one another—it was a staple of the cinema. This was the first time I'd seen it done in this way, as calculated and pitiless as a firing squad itself, no possibility to dissociate, no way to look someplace else. Stanley apparently wanted a last-minute reprieve for the condemned soldiers, a happy ending, because it was more commercial, and he wanted to make money. Now, twenty-five years later, he wanted Joker, the teenage hero of Hasford's novel *The Short-Timers* and of his still-untitled movie, to die. (He also wanted a Joker voice-over.) I didn't think so. "It's the Death of the Hero," he said, "it'll be so powerful, so *moving*." And he was genuinely moved by it. "We've seen it in *Homer*, Michael . . ."

I'd arrived for work in the late afternoon. "Ready for some serious brainstorming, Michael? You want a drink first?" I reflexively checked my watch. "How come all you heavy drinkers always look at your watches when somebody offers you a drink?"

Jim Thompson had made him nervous when they were working together on *The Killing*, a big guy in a dirty old raincoat, a terrific writer but a little too hard-boiled for Stanley's taste. He'd turn up for work carrying a bottle in a brown paper bag, but saying nothing about it—it was just there on the desk with no apology or comment—not at all interested in putting Stanley at ease except to offer him the bag, which Stanley declined, making no gestures whatever to any part of the Hollywood process, except maybe toward the money.

We were working that afternoon in the War Room, a large space on the ground floor which would have been airy if it weren't crammed with desks and computers and filing cabinets, long trestle tables littered with sketches, plans, contracts, hundreds of photographs of weapons, streets, pagodas, prostitutes, shrines, signs. (He'd taken three months, an entire summer, to go through his *Full Metal Jacket* contract with Warners, crawling up underneath the boilerplating to make sure there were no hidden viruses, checking the esoteric meanings of "force majeure," calling his lawyer Louis Blau in L.A. every hour, because Stanley hated surprises.) There were two sets of French doors opening onto the garden, part of which was fenced in to make sure that none of the dogs got to any of the cats. He kept the cats in this section of the house and fed them himself. While we talked he cleaned their litter boxes.

The American language of the Vietnam War gave him tremendous pleasure. "Michael, I need this scene finished most ricky-tick" (a variation on "I don't want it good, I want it Tuesday"), or "Michael, these pages you sent me today are Number Ten . . . In fact, I think they may even be Number *Twelve.*" One scene, where a bunch of Marines sit around in the evening eating C rations and talking (titled "C Rats With Andre" on the scene-by-scene file cards he kept) wasn't only too long, but too talky, boring, and a little sentimental. "Shouldn't there be some guy playing a *harmonica* in the back?" he said. One day we took a few of Stanley's guns over to a local gun club and fired at their range. It surprised him that someone who'd spent so much time in a war could be such a lousy shot. "Gee Michael, I'm beginning to wonder if you've got what it takes to carry a rifle in my beloved Corps."

The walls of his workrooms were one continuous shooting board; lists and schedules, names, dates, equipment, locations; except for one crowded wall, which seemed to be devoted to Stanley's investments.

He liked the way my pages looked; open spacing, agreeable format, good *font*, big enough for easy reading but never obtrusive. He was very complimentary about the dialogue. But he wanted the scenes shorter. "Tell me, Michael, did you ever see a movie that had too many good short scenes?"—a funny question from a director who loved long takes and long scenes, who was, in Anthony Lane's opinion, "almost insolent toward the demands of chronology," which wasn't meant as a compliment but should be, and referred perhaps to the leap across three million years in a single jump cut in *2001*, or the languorous protractions of eighteenth-century discourse held in rooms lit by candles in *Barry Lyndon*, every one of his films making its powerful assertion that pace is story as surely as character is destiny. He'd watched *The Godfather* again the night before, and was reluctantly suggesting for the tenth time that it was possibly the greatest movie ever made, and certainly the best cast.

"Your buddy Francis really hit the nail on the head with that one . . ." (Because Francis was another director, and a friend of mine, Stanley affected to regard him through a long lens.) "It was certainly better than *One from the Heart*."

"I loved *One from the Heart*," I said.

"Boy, Michael, you're so *loyal*. Anyway, what were we talking about?"

"Computers."

It drove him nuts that I didn't use one. This was 1983, pre-laptop. There were five computers in this room alone, all running, and he'd move from station to station to feed and manipulate data while we talked.

"Michael, listen to me: It's only a very limited, *arbitrary*, and simple series of commands that you just don't know yet. I mean, how hard can it be? The *police* use them."

"I know, Stanley, but . . ."

"Michael I'm telling you, *blah blah blah*," and "Michael, I swear to God *blah blah blah*. At least for *screenplays*" (a lesser form), "you're crazy not to use them."

He gave a demonstration to soften my Luddite heart and show me that I was only making more work for myself by resisting. He went to the computer that he was using to write the script. He typed, marked, cut, moved, pasted, while I faked interest. When he was finished with the routine, Christiane phoned to say that dinner was ready. As we left, I reminded him that he hadn't turned the computers off.

"They like to be left on," he said ironically, factually, tenderly.

I sometimes thought that he was ruled by his aversions, chief among them, worse than waste, haste, carelessness to details, hugging, and even germs, was bullshit in all its proliferating manifestations, subtle and gross, from the flabby political face telling lies on TV to the most private, much more devastating lies we tell ourselves. Culture lies were especially revolting. Hypocrisy was not some petty human foible, it was the corrupted essence of our predicament, which for Stanley was purely an existential predicament. In terms of narrative, since movies are stories, the most contemptible lie was sentimentality, and the most disgusting lie was sanctimoniousness.

Once a year he'd get the latest issue of *Maledicta*, a journal of scatological invective and insult, unashamedly incorrect, willfully scurrilous, and pretty funny, and read me the highlights.

"Hey Michael, what's The American Dream?

"I give."

"Ten million blacks swimming to Africa, with a Jew under each arm."

To which he added, "Don't worry, Michael. They don't mean us."

Since everybody talks about Stanley Kubrick's Eye, I'd like to say a word about his Ear: I've read often enough about his "suspicion of language," in books and critical pieces, and in the strangely rancorous tributes that followed his death, and yet it's always seemed obvious to me that language was one of the most striking things about his films. Whether cunningly, crushingly banal (a couple of "normal guys [getting] together to talk about world events in a normal sort of way," as Quilty incognito tells Humbert agonistes) or in manic bursts of frantic satire (inspired and encouraged, maybe childishly egged on, by Terry Southern and Peter Sellers), or starkly obscene, utterly cruel, sparing nobody's sensibilities; from yarblocko *nadsat* to the elaborate yet brutal locutions of the eighteenth century, to the vicious comedy of *Full Metal Jacket*, he was highly sensitive to literary mis-en-scène, completely susceptible to it. He wasn't merely unsuspicious of language, he was a believer, he had *faith* in it. Without it, dialogue was just talk.

Once he became his own man, he was drawn to his projects as much by the writing of the source material as by anything else, story was at least as alive in the voice as it was in the plot; I know this is true of *Lolita*, *A Clockwork Orange*, *Barry Lyndon*, and *Full Metal Jacket* (and if it didn't already exist in Stephen King, Stanley and Diane Johnson brilliantly invented it for *The Shining*), and *Eyes Wide Shut* carries the reflected refracted *written* essence of *Dream Novel*, no matter what Stanley did to the "story," after leaving it to season for nearly thirty years in his mind. He was always looking for the visual equivalents of what he'd first responded to when he'd read the book, and in that way paying some real respect to it.

Stanley didn't live in England because he disliked America, God knows; America was all he ever talked about. It was always on his mind, and in his blood. I'm not sure he even really knew he wasn't living in America all along, although he hadn't been there since 1968. In the days before satellite TV, he'd had relatives and friends send him tapes of American television—NFL games, *The Johnny Carson Show*, news broadcasts, and commercials, which he thought were, in their way, the most interesting films being made. (He'd tape his favorite commercials and recut them, just for the monkish exercise.) He was crazy about *The Simpsons* and *Seinfeld*, and he loved *Roseanne*, because it was funny and, he believed, the most authentic view of the country you could get without actually living there. "Gee, Stanley, you're a real man of the people," I said, and in his way, he was. He was fiercely unpretentious. He was exclusive, he had to be, but he wasn't a snob. It wasn't America he couldn't take. It was L.A.

He was walking into a Hollywood restaurant one night in 1955 as James Dean came out, stepped into the Porsche Spyder that had just been brought around by the parking valet, and drove off. Stanley remarked at the time how fast he was going.

He lived in Hollywood for three or four years and made two movies, *The Killing*, which got him a lot of attention, and *Paths of Glory*, which got him a lot of respect. He and his partner James B. Harris formed a small company. He went to a thousand meetings with Harris, *tummled* and *hondled*, read and wrote scripts, watched the big changes as star power, in the form of independent production companies, started breaking down the old studios, and wished all the time that he was in New York.

Harris told me that when they were making *Paths of Glory*, Stanley came to him with a new final scene, something to follow the execution of the three soldiers and make the ending less grim. A young German girl has been captured by the French, and they force her to sing for them in a tavern. They intend to humiliate her, but when she sings, her innocence and the suffering that they've all been through move them to tears of shame and humanity.

Stanley had just met a young German actress, Susanne Christiane, and was going out with her. "She was his girl-friend," Harris said. "He was really crazy about her, and he came to me with this scene he'd just written, and I said, Stanley, you can't just do this scene so your girlfriend can be in the movie." But Stanley had his way, and gave the film an unforgettable ending. The actress was incredible. Then she and Stanley got married, and the marriage lasted forty years. Harris laughed. "Boy, was I wrong."

Stanley could hardly fail to notice that very few direc-tors had anything close to autonomy on their pictures. He said the way the studios were run in the fifties made him think of Clemenceau's remark about the Allies winning World War I because our generals were marginally less stu-pid than their generals. He was determined to find some way to succeed there, because he didn't know where else he could make movies. His ambition was spectacular, he had talent and confidence, a steely brain and huge brass balls. He saw clearly that on every picture someone had to be in charge, and figured that it might as well be him.

He told me that he owed it all to Kirk Douglas. Dou-glas once called Stanley "a talented shit," and this may be one of the nicer things he said about him. He'd starred in *Paths of Glory*, and even though he'd done himself a lot of good by it, I imagine that he felt Stanley owed him, and would be grateful and pliant when he hired him to replace Anthony Mann after three weeks of shooting on *Spartacus*. The script had been written by Dalton Trumbo, who was still blacklisted in 1958, and when the producers agonized over whether they dared give him the credit or not, Stanley suggested that they solve the problem by giving the writing credit to *him*. (Douglas says that Stanley never wrote one word of that script, but I doubt this. Laurence Olivier's Crassus is the most complex character ever to appear in an epic genre film, almost Shakespearean, and I'm sure Stanley wrote and otherwise informed a lot of those scenes. I *don't* think he wrote lines like, "Get up, Spartacus, you Thracian dog.") Kirk Douglas (and this is rich) was offended by Stanley's *chutzpah*.

But specifically, conclusively, it was Kirk on horseback and Stanley on foot, just about to shoot a scene and having yet another of their violent disagreements. Kirk rode his white freedom-fighter stallion into Stanley to make his point, which was that he was the star *and* the producer, turning his horse's flank against Stanley, pushing him back farther and farther to drive it home again, then riding away, leaving Stanley standing in the dust, furious and humiliated, as one of the wise guys on the crew walks by and says, "Remember Stanley—*The play's the thing.*"

The only other places he knew of to make movies in were New York and London, and New York was too hard, and too expensive. That's how he became English Stanley, and why he made all his movies there, most of them within an hour's drive of his house. The English work ethic drove him nuts. The crew would call him "Squire" on the set, and he got so pissed off at their endless tea breaks that he wanted to surreptitiously film them when he was shooting *Lolita* there in 1960. He said, "England's a place where it's much more difficult to *buy* something than to *sell* something." He once asked me if I'd mind moving with my family to Vancouver for a year to check it out for him, and he heard Sydney was a great place, maybe I could try that out for him too, but he liked England, it suited his family and it suited him, living and working and making telephone calls in his great house, his multi-gated manor, his estate, his *park*. And anyway, if he'd lived in America, it would have been in such a house, used in the same way, as a studio, a citadel, a monastery, a controlled Stanley Kubrick environment, so what difference did it make which country it was in?

4

Gentiles don't know how to worry.

—Stanley Kubrick

I DON'T WANT TO GIVE THE IMPRESSION that I didn't get extremely irritated, that I never thought he was a cheap prick, or that his lack of trust wasn't sometimes obstructive and less than wholesome, that his demands and requirements weren't just *too much.* Nothing got between the dog and his meat, somewhere it was that basic—I only just hesitate to say primitive. It was definitely unobstructed; you'd have to be Herman Melville to transmit the full strength of Stanley's will, My Way or The Highway, yet he rarely raised his voice. It was hard to know whether he was just supernaturally focused or utterly fixated. "What is it they say, Michael—if something can go wrong, it will?" Vigilance wasn't enough, preemption was the only way to go. Don't think just because you've known a few control freaks in your time that you can imagine what Stanley Kubrick was like.

Tony Frewin and Leon Vitali, who'd been working as Stanley's assistants for years, said there was a staff joke about the one phrase you would never hear at Childwick Bury, and a week after Stanley's death someone actually said it to them. It went, "Use your own judgment, and don't bother me with the details." His concerns ran from the ethereal-aesthetic through the technical to the crudely logistical, no detail too mundane, all the way down to stationery and paper clips.

We know that even though he had a pilot's license, he'd stopped flying altogether by 1960, allegedly after monitoring the air controllers at La Guardia Airport. I used to kid him about oversubscribing to the germ theory, and he'd go on various health kicks as long as they didn't require any effort, like an aspirin a day, and vitamin C in the form of Redoxon, an English fizzy tablet in various flavors, "very pleasant-tasting," upgraded to "delicious," and invoking scientific opinion, "I mean Michael, it's *Linus Pauling*. He certainly ought to know what he's talking about," figuring, anyway, "At the worst, you're only wasting your money."

He had more compartments in his head than anyone I ever knew, he would open or close them selectively to the people he was working with, or to each of his friends; the one with the money in it, the one where he kept all his toys, the one where he kept his most personal things, like his hopes and his fears, that sort of thing, and whatever he loved most besides work, his family and friends, his dogs and cats. And however adroitly he manipulated the doors to those compartments, now open, now closed, essentially Stanley was a very open guy. Still, none of those compartments ever sprang open accidentally.

Beyond those compartments, and governing them, was a capability to take his intelligence up or down as circumstances required, without ever being either obscure or patronizing, a rather beautiful quality of mind.

I once told Stanley William Burroughs's line, "A paranoid-schizophrenic is a guy who just found out what's going on," and he took it to his heart. "Wait a minute wait a minute . . . I've gotta write that down." He put it into wide release, telling it to everyone he knew, and I think it was mostly because he was so pleased to find himself of one mind with someone he admired as much as Burroughs. "What is it they say, Michael: What one has thought so often, but never said so well?"

Stanley would have said it was cash, but I think the most perishable element in the making of a movie is reverence. On most pictures it rarely survives the first day of shooting, but in Stanley's case it had a life of its own. You can follow its career over the course of a series of interviews, usually but not always with actors, normally spanning a couple of years: They're so honored to be working with Stanley, they'd do anything in the world to work with Stanley, such a privilege they'd work with Stanley for free. And then they work with Stanley and go through hells that nothing in their careers could have prepared them for, they think they must have been mad to get involved, they think that they'd die before they would ever work with him again, that fixated maniac; and when it's all behind them and the profound fatigue of so much intensity has worn off, they'd do anything in the world to work for him again. For the rest of their professional lives they long to work with someone who cared the way Stanley did, someone they could learn from. They look for someone to respect the way they'd come to respect him, but they can never find anybody. Their received fictionalized show-business reverence has been chastened and reborn as real reverence. I've heard this story so many times.

He'd been looking all day at hundreds of audition tapes sent in from all over America and England in response to the public casting call for *Full Metal Jacket.*

"Some of them are interesting. Most of them are terrible. Oh well, I suppose I can always wipe the tapes and use them to record football on." Like this was the first he'd thought of it.

Stanley was in his Low Road mode for *Full Metal Jacket.* "I only want people working on this one that no one else will hire, or, if they hired them, would never dream of hiring them again." This was of course Kubrickian misanthropic hyperbole, muttered privately to me, because he could never, would never, work with anyone less than the best, even if that meant educating them all, "correcting" them, as Grady called it in *The Shining.* And he started in on actors and all the problems they bring, not forgetting to sing a few choruses, without much conviction, of his old song about *actors* being to blame for the number of takes he was always forced to do. On *Barry Lyndon,* Marisa Berenson had a line, *We're taking the children for a ride to the village. We'll be back in time for tea.* "And Marisa couldn't *say* it. We must have done fifty on that one alone."

We talked a lot about actors for *Full Metal Jacket.* He couldn't wait to find out who would play Sergeant Hartman, the demon drill instructor, "it's such a fantastic part." We talked about Robert De Niro, but Stanley thought the audience would feel cheated when the character's killed off in the first hour. Then he was thinking about Ed Harris, but Harris wasn't interested because, "Get this Michael. He wants to take a *year off!*. . . Hey, I know! What about Richard Benjamin? He'd be perfect, Michael, ha ha ha ha . . ."

He didn't exactly mutter the word "actors" under his breath like a curse, but he definitely thought of them as wild cards, something to be overcome with difficulty. They were so lazy about learning their lines, were so often otherwise unprepared, so capricious, so childlike, and the younger ones were completely spoiled. There was even something mysterious, and to him a little freakish, about anybody who could and would stand up in front of other people to assume and express emotions at will, sometimes to the point of tears.

"I don't know," I said. "I have to tell you, I really like actors."

"That's because you don't have to pay them, Michael."

One of the sweetest things anybody ever said about Stanley, and one of the truest, was something Matthew Modine told Stanley's biographer Vincent LoBrutto:

"He's probably the most heartfelt person I ever met. It's hard for him, being from the Bronx with that neighborhood mentality, and he tries to cover it up. Right underneath that veneer is a very loving, conscientious man, who doesn't like pain, who doesn't like to see humans suffering or animals suffering. I was really surprised by the man."

This from a guy who really suffered for most of the year that he was in London shooting *Full Metal Jacket*, as part of an ensemble of young actors, some of them hardly actors at all, who had only the most rudimentary sense of what Stanley actually meant by "knowing your lines"; by which he meant that you had to know them so completely that there were no other possible lines anywhere in your head, and certainly no lines of your own, unless you were Peter Sellers or Lee Ermey. They were a jolly enthusiastic crew, some very talented, some not, all thrilled to be in a Stanley Kubrick movie—I think they all saw blue skies and high times ahead—but there was a plateau of discipline that they couldn't have known existed before. Stanley showed them, and it hurt.

Then there was a break in the shooting of almost five months after Lee Ermey smashed up his car late one night and broke all his ribs on one side. Some of the cast had other jobs lined up and had to juggle, while they sat and waited in London, going to the theater five and six times a week, and tried to keep some kind of edge. Vincent D'Onofrio had gained forty or fifty pounds to play Leonard, and he had to keep it on through all those idle months. A few of them with their wives and girlfriends would come to our apartment for dinner, and they were all flipping out. They believed that Stanley only asked me to the set on the rare days when there were no foreseeable glitches, because he didn't want me to hear the way he spoke to them. When I went to the set, they'd come over to me between takes, search my face for a clue, confused and half-mutinous, and then Stanley would walk by and say something like, "Don't talk to my actors, Michael."

I have no idea what really went on for Stanley with actors. I do know that it was his belief, or his prevailing hunch, that actors were really only working when film was running. If he had any preconceptions about what he wanted them to be doing, he kept them to himself. Maybe actors were essentially visuals for Stanley, like Alfred Hitchcock and his blondes. Stanley said he didn't like Hitchcock much, "all that phony rear-projection," but they had a lot in common. I was always impressed by what Hitchcock did with, or *to*, James Stewart in *Vertigo*, ruthlessly (but far more subtly than Carl Dreyer making Falconetti kneel on cobblestones all night to experience the suffering of Joan of Arc) drawing a performance out of him that was so sweaty, tortured, and unwholesome that, if Stewart knew he'd had any of *that* in him, he would have done anything in the world to conceal it. I think that Stanley did something like this with just about every actor he ever worked with.

Nor could I explain that strange irresistible requirement he had for pushing his actors as far beyond a "naturalistic" style as he could get them to go, and often selecting their most extreme, awkward, emotionally confusing work for his final cut. The *peculiarity* of it—George C. Scott, Patrick McGee, and Jack Nicholson, just to pick the most blinding examples. Scott complained publicly that Stanley not only directed him way over the top but chose the most overwrought takes for the final cut, while Nicholson's performance turned *The Shining* into a movie that largely failed as a genre piece but worked unforgettably on levels where it didn't matter that there was a huge movie star and great actor on the premises or not. (Nicholson did some of his greatest work, and his very worst, in *The Shining*, and the same could be said of the director.) "That was much more real," Stanley told him after a take. "But it isn't interesting." Even the biggest stars knew what it was like to be a pawn in Stanley's game, to stare helplessly at the sheer North Face of Stanley's resolve, "That was really terrific. Let's go again." Of all the things I could say about Stanley, the best of them is that when you worked for him, you earned your salary.

They'd come to him for direction, and he'd send them back to work to find out for themselves. When Malcolm McDowell asked, he told him, "Malcolm, I'm not RADA. I hired *you* to do the acting." He was preparing a scene for *Spartacus* in which Laurence Olivier and Nina Foch are sitting in their seats above the arena waiting for the gladiators to enter and fight to the death, and Nina Foch asked him for motivation. "What am I doing, Stanley?" she asked, and Stanley said, "You're sitting here with Larry waiting for the gladiators to come out."

The usual MO was for him to become incredibly close to actors during shooting, and then to never see them again. A lot of actors were terribly hurt by this. There's no question that the affection he felt for them and the inspiration he extended to them were genuine, and this made the break even more painful. For Stanley's part, I never heard him speak of an actor, even ones who had given him a hard time or been "disloyal" once the film came out, with anything but affection, like a family member who'd gone off, dispelled into some new career phase, even if it was oblivion.

5

He told me once that if he hadn't become a director he might have liked being a conductor. "They get to play the whole orchestra, and they get plenty of exercise," he said, waving his arms a bit, "and most of them live to be really old."

As I write this, the release of his last film is two months away. Only a few people have seen it, and already the entertainment media is holding itself ready to be shocked and offended, or pretending to. "What's new?" Stanley would have said, as if it hardly warranted the question mark. He'd begun planning the publicity campaign before he'd finished the final cut of the film, but I'm sure that he thought about it for years. Some people seem to think that he's controlling it from the grave. It's inconceivable to anyone who knew him that an energy like that could stop just because death has occurred, that it isn't going on in some form, circulating. This very book is evidence of that, since it grew from a piece that he wanted me to write about him, specifically for *Vanity Fair*, to coincide with the opening of *Eyes Wide Shut*.

In the two and a half years between the time that I declined to wash and rinse for fun, and the moment that he finished editing, we talked only a few times. He was shooting for most of it; he said it was going great, no matter what I might have heard. He was crazy about his stars, impressed with their professionalism and their energy; he said they energized the whole crew and made his job a lot easier. The only other actor I ever heard him speak quite that way about was James Mason, and that was on the day after Mason died.

In the beginning of January my wife and I received a gift from him, a book of photographs by Jacques Henri Lartigue. It was a Seasons Greetings present, the first we'd had in three years, since he'd gone into production.

"That was nice of him," my wife said. She'd always liked Stanley.

"Yes, it was," I said, thinking, *I wonder what he wants.*

The calls started up again, every couple of days, longer and longer. He sounded terrific, it was great to be on the blower with him again. For the first time since I'd known him, he actually asked me if there was some time of day that was better for me than others, so we did most of the talking in the mornings, his afternoons: Did I happen to see Norman Mailer's piece in *The New York Review of Books* about Tom Wolfe? *Brilliant, he must be pretty old now, Michael, but what passion*, and, *I hear your buddy Francis just won a bundle from Warner Bros. in a lawsuit*, and, *Somebody ought to write a book about Bill Clinton and call it, "He's Got to Have It."*

Then, one morning, "Hey Michael (already laughing), I've had a great idea! How'd you like to write the *exclusive* piece on *Eyes Wide Shut* for *Vanity Fair?*"

I didn't know. I was already working on something, and besides, I hadn't written a magazine piece in twenty years.

"Listen, it'll be fun . . . you come over for a week, I'll show you the movie, you can talk to Tom and Nicole, *interview* me . . . wouldn't you like to do that Michael?"

"I wouldn't know what to ask you."

"That's all right, I'll write all the questions . . . it'll be the only piece about the movie, you know, Michael, a really *classy* piece of P.R." (yuk yuk yuk), and, "You're the only one who can do it right," and, "It's perfect for you."

I said that since it was him I'd think about it, look into it. I decided to do it, and called him.

"Gee that's terrific, Michael. That makes me very happy."

"Me too, Stanley. Now you'll find out what I really think of you."

Problems arose, as I'd told Graydon Carter, the editor of *Vanity Fair*, they would. Stanley called to ask me what I meant by the word "exclusive," and I told him I'd never used the word, he had; what did *he* mean by "exclusive"? Then he called in extreme distress and said that he couldn't possibly show me the movie in time for my deadline, there was looping to be done and the music wasn't finished, lots of small technical fixes on color and sound, but it wasn't ready to show; would I show work that wasn't finished? He *had* to show it to Tom and Nicole because they had to sign nudity releases, and to Terry Semmel and Bob Daly of Warner Bros., but he *hated* it that he had to, and I could hear it in his voice that he did. But once that screening was over, and the response to it was so strong, he relented.

"All right, Michael. Let me see." Then we talked about Hemingway again, how you could never break that prose down into components that could be studied and examined and qualified and expect it to tell you how it worked in the magical way that it did.

On the Friday before he died, I was driving to Vermont on the New York State Thruway when my cell phone rang.

"Michael, can you drive and talk?"

"Yes Stanley. And chew gum."

"No, I mean, is it *legal*?"

He told me it would be all right if I came over in two weeks to look at the movie and "interview" him. When I asked him if this was his last word on the subject he laughed and said, "Maybe."

Then he told me about a friend of his, a studio head who'd just bought an apartment in New York. He told me how much he'd paid for it, and said that he was the first Jew ever admitted to the building.

"Can you believe that? What is it, 1999? And they never let a Jew in there before?"

In Holland, he'd heard, there was a football team called Ajax that had once had a Jewish player, and ever since then, Dutch skinheads would go to all the team's matches and make a loud hissing noise, meant to represent the sound of gas escaping into the death chambers. "And that's *Holland*, Michael. A *civilized* country." Laughing.

We talked for something like a hundred miles, from before Utica until my exit at Albany. I told him I needed both hands now, and that I'd call him when I got home on Sunday.

All the things that people believe they know about Stanley they get from the press, and the entertainment press at that.

Almost none of these reporters ever met him, because he thought you had to be crazy to do interviews unless you had a picture coming out, and even then it had to be very carefully managed. It wasn't personal with him, but I think it became personal for a lot of them. They work hard, much too hard, the belt is moving faster and faster, carrying increasingly empty forms, silly and brutal and thankfully evanescent entertainments. You can't go to the movies anymore without slipping in all the Pavlovian drool running down the aisles, big show-business Manifest. This is the world that Stanley chose to become a master of, and one of the ways he did it was by keeping himself to himself. So I can understand, in a time when so many celebrities are so eager to hurl themselves into our headlights, why anyone who doesn't want to talk with the entertainment press might seem eccentric, reclusive, and misanthropic; crazy, autocratic, and humorless; cold and phobic and arrogant.

But I must say that a lot of people took it hard when he died; people he'd known, some of them, for forty years, or people he hadn't seen in a decade; certainly his family, since he'd been a loving husband and father—amazing, the number of people who loved him, and the way they loved him, and the size of the hole he made in our lives by dying. He was so alive to us that it was hard to believe he was dead, and then there was that other thing ("We've seen it in Homer, Michael"), people regarding their dead heroes and thinking, If it can do this to him, imagine what it can do to us.

He'd never talk about his movies while he was making them, and he didn't like talking about them afterward very much, even to friends, except maybe to mention the grosses. Most of all, he didn't want to talk about their "meaning," because he believed so completely in their meaning that to try and talk about it could only spoil it for him. He might tell you *how* he did it, but never why. An arch-materialist (maybe), and an artist of the material world, I think he made the single most inspired spiritual image in all of film, the Star Child watching with equanimity the timeless empty galaxies of existence-after-existence, waiting patiently once again to be born. Somebody asked him how he ever thought of the ending of *2001.* "I don't know," he said. "How does anybody ever think of anything?"

Postscript: *Eyes Wide Shut*

A COUPLE OF DAYS after Stanley's funeral, the London *Times* ran a story about a sixty-seven-year-old former house-keeper for the Kubrick family named Betty Compton, who was planning a memoir. "He was eccentric and paranoid," she said, "but he was not a lunatic." She added, "If you didn't patronize him, he was great to work with." I found this to be true.

The following week, Frederic Raphael, Stanley's palpably unhappy collaborator on the screenplay for *Eyes Wide Shut*, had the proposal for *his* memoir on publishers' desks. The book that swiftly followed made a display that was hard for a lot people to take. It wasn't just that it was so antagonistic to Stanley, or even that it was so bitter and self-humiliating, but that it was so unfailingly patronizing. Stanley, we gather, hadn't been sufficiently deferential to Raphael's credentials, to his academic attainments and his immense store of knowledge, his often unfortunate command of foreign words and phrases and the insolent presumption of superiority that came along with it all, however unentitled. We read of Stanley the tyrant, Stanley the obsessive perfectionist, cold Stanley, secretive Stanley, un-*helpful* Stanley, and a new one—particularly distasteful because it was so gratuitously trumped up as to look like mere projection—Stanley the self-hating Jew.

"They're either at your throat or they're at your feet, " Stanley said, recalling a catchphrase that was current in European diplomatic circles after the Second World War. Then, it referred to the Germans; now, he was talking about critics and commentators on the culture in general, entertainment journalists: high-, low-, but mostly middlebrow, generally contentious and misinformed, sometimes flagrantly intellectual media mavens. Whenever he possibly could he'd try and put one of them in his pocket, so to speak (there are no ex–chess masters), but the deformed perception of him among so many of them, and the fixated way that it operated, was at best uncomfortable for him, even though he was aware that by being the way he was, he was only nourishing it. He understood both the principle of complete cover and the cost of it. Nevertheless, he was a sensitive guy (I can hardly believe that I feel the need to say this, and so explicitly), and his feelings could be hurt. He wasn't especially touchy; it's hard to imagine him sulking, or brooding about anything other than work. He wasn't fragile as glass, and the change of seasons didn't make him weep, but stupidity and injustice hurt his feelings, and it wasn't even as personal as you might think.

When I first knew Stanley, I told him that when I had come to New York in the early sixties I worked briefly as the film critic (unpaid) of a magazine called *The New Leader*. ("You mean they didn't pay you *anything*?" "They paid for the movie tickets." "Gee, Michael . . . Did you at least have a percentage of the profits? An expense account? *Luncheon vouchers?*") I told him that one of the movies I'd reviewed had been *Lolita*, so naturally he called someone in New York and had them go down into the catacombs beneath the Public Library to find the review and send it to him. He liked it. I'd given it a rave. I gave it a much better review than Stanley himself did.

I was useless as a critic. I had followed Manny Farber at the magazine, one of the best of all writers on movies, as I was reminded when an expanded collection of his criticism called *Negative Space* was published in 1998. I was out of my element, and out of my depth. My reviews weren't very good to begin with—I seem to remember claiming that a Japanese movie called *The Island* was such a moving experience that I didn't realize until it was over that there hadn't been a word of spoken dialogue—and I made matters worse by disliking a series of fashionable (for five minutes) European films, and then by falling for a bunch of Hollywood movies that were nothing more than studio product that looked good, or were true-to-the-code genre pictures, or that otherwise amused me. (Most of the films from all these categories, foreign and domestic, have vanished, gone like they'd never been made.) I didn't last very long, less than a year, but in that short time I came to hate going to the movies, an incredible thing for someone who before then had never seen a movie that he didn't like.

I remember this whenever I think about the lives that critics must lead, particularly movie critics, and even more particularly the old-school cineasts, the back-of-the-book veterans who still write film criticism after forty years and more, yet without having developed light and playful minds; telling other people where they went wrong, living under the day-to-day strain of having to come up with another super-lative, one more pejorative, while still maintaining their credibility. And I know, because I've been there, that there is a hellworld where you're always expected to have an opin-ion about everything all the time: a judgment, a take—a "view," in the most ordinary sense of the word.

"I've been reading some of these reviews," Stanley said, "and boy, Michael . . . remember that old radio program, *It Pays to Be Ignorant?*" This was after *Full Metal Jacket* opened, and he was warming to a few remarks about spe-cific critics. "Oh well anyway, at least they try and spell my name right," he said, looking on the up side.

As a friend of his, I never used to care that much when I'd read some of the crap that they wrote about him, but now that he's dead, I have to say, it upsets me. Of course, it's always painful to see a great artist belittled by fools, simply because of their mean, confused, negative conjectures, misconception layered upon misconception, awesomely committed to misconception. It can never turn out well when a square takes a hipster for his subject. Essentially incapable of regarding him as anything other than the weird phobic controlling maniac of fable more than legend, they hold stubbornly, I would even say stupidly, to their assumptions, often objecting to him personally, to his secrecy and his silence and even his wealth. (There was even some suspicious grousing about his "mysterious" death, as though the great elusive could never be overtaken by anything as prosaic as a heart attack.) Accepting and circulating the presumptions about Stanley's pathology, they have themselves acquired a pathological dislike of him and his work. Never mind for the moment that many of them are actually good critics, people I've read for years and continue to read. They get that Stanley bit between their teeth, and they're off like a bugaboo strapped to a hobbyhorse.

The strangely contentious and extremely disrespectful tone that lurked inside so many of the obituaries and tributes was unpleasant to the many people who loved Stanley, but not surprising. Then *Eyes Wide Shut* came out, and then the reviews, and the inescapable flood of what used to be called "think pieces": *The New Yorker*, *The New York Times* (with the notable exception of Janet Maslin, whose passionate appreciation of the film was rumored to have been the catalyst for her resignation from that paper), *The New York*

Review of Books, *The New Republic*, same old same old, *Ill Seen Ill Said.* There aren't many spectacles more dispiriting than this one: the culture-critical smart set, united in aversion, dreadfully putting on their thinking caps.

As a not so pure product of the sixties, I've often wondered whether over the long run the sexual freedom of those years didn't numb more genitals than it inflamed, more than all the prohibitions of all the decades that went before. The actual realization, after so much collective longing, of a genuine liberation of erotic impulse and expression pumped a marvelous vitality into the culture; many modes and views that were (allegedly) undreamed of a generation before, or even a year before, were out there frolicking in the open air, swimming naked in the mainstream, visible, televised, explicit, rampant. But what if freedom *isn't* just another word for nothing left to lose, but something that's lost whenever you mistake a carnal matter for a spiritual matter? If there was a liberation thirty years ago, why now all this confusion, rancor, pornography?

The misbegotten and briefly famous media campaign for *Eyes Wide Shut* is already forgotten, except by entertainment marketing professionals, and then only for the devastation of its backfire. There were no fast-food tie-ins, but no movie can open any longer without an appeal to whatever is less than wholesome in us. This one opened behind sex and supercelebrity, although not even Tom Cruise could save it as product, and sex was its downfall. It was a bad idea in this salacious climate to toy with people's expectations by suggesting that *Eyes Wide Shut* was going to be the sexiest movie ever made, a *Last Tango in Paris* for our sex-drunk times, instead of telling the extremely risky truth and saying that it was merely one of the most beautiful.

"Art-phobia is now the dominant sensibility of the official culture, and art-phobia annihilated Stanley Kubrick's autumnal work," Lee Siegel wrote in *Harper's* magazine a couple of months after the debacle, eloquently taking the words right out of my mouth, and speaking for what he believes to be a great film. Bravely, he continues, "Genuine art makes you stake your credulity on the patently counterfeit," a gambit he claims the critics didn't even consider, let alone dare. (Film critics insensible to mis-en-scène are not a recent phenomenon; no one who remembers Bosley Crowther, chief critic of *The New York Times* from the forties well into the sixties, can think that art-phobia in "high places" is new.) "For they fear that if they surrender themselves to the work's strangeness, they will seem vulnerable and naive and intellectually unreliable." Instead of responding to the movie, they responded to the hype, trashing the movie both as a commodity and an entertainment. Siegel goes on in understandable indignation to explain how a film so ravishing and benign and certainly strange could have fallen through so many cracks in the culture.

Stanley was hardly blameless in this, and I suppose it's possible that if he thought he could get away with it, at this time and in this country, then maybe he *was* out of it. We can take it as a given that he controlled the publicity and marketing strategies until the hour that he died. I don't know who became the commander afterward, or whether it was a shared command, but there was an excessive use of firepower, and many missed targets, and the collateral damage was all to the movie. Some critics loved it, but most, often speaking for the public, wrote so scornfully that it was difficult to keep from forming a snotty attitude myself, one that said that people who love movies love Stanley's movies, and those who don't, don't.

After busting him all these years for his nihilism, they busted him now for his belief, often with a blend of stridency, cynicism, and pofaced hypocrisy: "Kubrick: A Sadness" (boo hoo), from *The New Republic*, and "A stiff, alas" (oh boy oh boy), from *The New Yorker*. The tears were positively crocodilian, and more than one commentator, looking back a few months later on many of those first reviews, remarked on the disagreeable aura of self-congratulation that played so solemnly through them. (One critic spoke of Stanley's "brutal voyeurism," but it was only voyeurism, and anyway, could he direct me to a director who *isn't* a voyeur?) They wrote as if they'd been cheated; and they wrote facetiously, condescendingly, insultingly. But you can't cheat an honest man, and I'm fairly certain that you can't insult a work of art. All you can do is damage its reputation at a decisive moment, and seriously hurt its box-office.

Expecting sex, promised sex in writing, critics and commentators and audiences wanted sex. They were outraged that the orgy didn't turn out to be the Fuckorama of their not unreasonable expectations, that the stars didn't get all the way down so we could watch. What they got instead was an eroticism so deeply embedded in memory and imagination that the more physical it becomes, the less erotic. They got the sex that's indivisible from death, and an orgy that was certainly fleshly enough, yet anaphrodisiac, liturgical. Tom Cruise wanders the streets of New York (static and underpopulated streets, according to the critical consensus) for the better part of two days and nights, and except for one time, with his wife and offscreen, can't manage to get laid; not with the squirming sirens that he meets at a party (the stimulating Gayle and the lovely Nuala, who spells her name out for him and makes it sound like a new word for pleasure), not with a beautiful, kindhearted hooker (he pays her anyway) or a sweet and possibly simpleminded nymphet paradigm of natural sex, not even at an orgy, even though everywhere he goes, everything that moves comes on to him, man, woman, and child.

Neither, in spite of a few dark shadows and some spooky music, did they get the advertised thriller. Instead, they got mystery, much more problematic, a film of curious incident and haunting color, of city streets at night that look like they've had a spell put on them, of masks and Christmas trees, of ringing telephones and flunkies approaching with requests from their masters, apparent interruptions that are really cues for the next passage to begin. The subject isn't sex and thrills but marriage and fidelity; Fidelio is the password and the presiding spirit of the piece.

In the Mozart comedies (so called), the frantic unfunny farce on the stage tells one story while the music tells the real one. It's the same in each of them, those incomparable poems of fidelity and honor struggling for parity in a fickle, whorish world; chastity besieged and betrayed, a lover's faith tossed on the table like stakes in a careless wager, *Cosi Fan Tutte;* very amusing, for sadists and cynics at any rate, and irresistible to artists. Schnitzler caught the mordant gist of it in *Traumnovelle*, and Stanley transposed it to a far warmer key, changing its meanings. It's not like *Don Giovanni* at all, although there's an *hommage* to the Don in the character of Sandor Szavost (Stanley's little Hungarian joke, played with cheesy charm by Sky Dumont). *Eyes Wide Shut* is much more like *The Magic Flute*, a fairy tale, with a dangerous, possibly ethereal quest successfully accomplished, a curse lifted, and the semblance of a happy ending. And like the best fairy tales, enchantment provides the propulsion, and death is the ballast. The only Mozart actually on the sound track is from the *Requiem*.

In place of the fastidious and unsettling creepiness of *Traumnovelle* (which isn't the sexiest novella ever written, but one of the most disturbing), Stanley created a deep charm that hardly exists in the text, but that can be found in the films of Lubitsch, Ophuls, and von Sternberg, a couple of dreamy Europeans and an inspired pretender. This alone was enough to set the New York quadrant smirking. Complaining, in so many words, that like all of his movies, *Eyes Wide Shut* didn't keep telling them what they were supposed to be feeling, they said that it was without feeling. Because it was in a style they hadn't seen before, they said that it had no style. (Or, in one case, objected that it was "stylized," as though stylization had suddenly become unacceptable in film.) They even said that it didn't have a story, but it did, and a good one, the one about the man who loved his wife.

Two camps have always formed around each of Stanley's movies, and no one in either camp could ever imagine what the other camp thought it was seeing. A lot of people were (and remain) indignant over *2001* and what they considered its hippy-dippy obfuscations. *Barry Lyndon* was written off as nothing more than a coffee-table movie, a day at the Prado without lunch. *A Clockwork Orange* was a moral abomination altogether, while a decade before, *Dr. Strangelove* was felt to be an unspeakable breach of etiquette. In the case of *Eyes Wide Shut* the camps were made up of people who knew within minutes that they were watching a dream film and those who didn't. Grudgingly conceding that Stanley possessed great imagination, they could never see how fanciful that imagination always was.

I have no idea how much of *Eyes Wide Shut* is meant to be taken literally as a dream, or a string of occurrences on the road running in and out of a dream, or a story with no logic but dream logic. Stanley always spoke of movies as dreams, dreams about dreams, including daydreams and nightmares (although I don't think he ever spoke of them as *only* dreams), and never made any distinction—this is the kind of materialist I think he really was—between a dream and a vision. But the very word "dream," and the activity it represents, have become gruesomely devalued by television, where when they speak of dreams they mostly mean some forlorn wish they want fulfilled, feel *entitled* to have fulfilled, something grossly material and equally impossible, nothing like a dream at all.

In *Eyes Wide Shut*, the Shostakovich waltz begins, a melancholy pastiche of a waltz, like a rose with a canker in it, as Alice steps between two pillars and lets her dress fall to the floor, in an apartment that was considered by some to be much too opulent, *unimaginably* opulent, for a New York doctor and his wife to be able to afford. Nevertheless they move around it as if they own the place, joined in something that would immediately be identified as domestic intimacy if this weren't a Stanley Kubrick film. Not concerned with blood and iron this time, or conflict on an international or cosmic scale, Stanley was in the mood for love, and he made a movie that was all for love, a high comedy about a couple crossing that sector of the connubial minefield where the devices are especially well buried. He turned his fixated gaze upon a conjugal arrangement composed of trust and complacency in equal measure that is about to be tested in the fire.

Dr. Bill Harford can tell his wife that she looks perfect without even looking at her because he loves her and he *knows* that she's perfect; it's one of the things about her that he takes for granted. He asks her if she's seen his wallet (the magic wallet that will produce thousands of dollars over the next three nights, and contains his amulet, the New York State Medical Board card, which will open many doors and relax many suspicions; it's okay, he's a doctor). She tells him that his wallet is on the bedside table. She removes her glasses, he turns off the waltz, and they step out into the highly eroticized, boundlessly suggestive New York Yuletide night.

According to the story, there was a fir tree in Eden that died when Eve ate the apple, and flowered again at the Nativity. And Stanley, with his German family connections, European sensibility, and wide voracious reading, must have come across the legend of Count Otto, called "Stone Heart" by his subjects because he never loved a woman, until he met the supernaturally beautiful Queen of the Fairies. She became his consort, and brought as her dowry a Christmas tree hung with gems and golden daggers, and said that she would be his just as long as he never uttered the word "death," which wasn't long.

There's a Christmas tree in Bill and Alice's apartment, there's a Christmas tree in the room where a presumably Jewish patient of Bill's has just died (and where the bereaved daughter devours Bill with hungry kisses as she embraces him at the feet of her father's corpse), and in the apartment of the prostitute whom Bill encounters in his downtown wanderings. (The music in this scene is "I Got It Bad and That Ain't Good." We find out later that she's HIV positive, and that Bill dodged a bullet by not fucking her. Good thing his cell phone rang.) A tree stands in the foyer of Victor Ziegler's town house, which looks like the manger where Mammon was born, and where a dream party is going on, more of a midwinter Saturnalia than a Christmas party. There's a tree in almost every room in the movie, except in the estate where the orgy is held, and that's surrounded by pines. There's one in Bill's office and another in the hospital where he goes to view the body of the mysterious woman who may have given her life for his, or who may have just been a hooker with a drug problem, "The one with the great tits who OD'd in my bathroom," as Victor so tenderly says later, when the mask falls off and his monster leaves its box.

Watching *Eyes Wide Shut*, I remembered the producer of some of the most successful action movies of the eighties, who said that he didn't want any women in his pictures unless they were either naked or dead. The few women who aren't already naked in *Eyes Wide Shut* are ready to become naked with only a glance from Bill; their clothing is just another illusion. And while there's only one dead woman in the story, there are steaming succubi and hungry animae and women who seem to look at Death as the guy they're really interested in; they're hot to go and they want to take somebody with them.

"Don't you want to go where the rainbow ends?" Gayle and Nuala ask Bill at the party. As far as they're concerned, it ends in bed with them, but he is called away, "summoned." (He doesn't find it later in Rainbow Fashions either, the comically sordid and utterly magical costume shop where Mr. Milich, a remarkable relic of old Europe, is doing his thing: *"What on earth is going on here?"* he bellows in mock outrage, knowing exactly what is going on. When he uncovers the two fantastical Japanese men dressed only in wigs and bikini briefs panting after his underage daughter, he cries, "Have you no sense of decency?" Then he sells her to them.)

What happens at the Christmas party, and over the next couple of nights, is all in consequence of Bill leaving his wife for a minute to follow the elusive and somewhat devilish Nick Nightingale (a great fairy-tale name), a med-school dropout and piano player for all occasions. Then *he's* summoned away, vanishes, and as Bill negotiates his perilous way between lascivious Gayle and tantalizing Nuala, Alice waltzes with her eager Hungarian. As Bill looks with professional detachment at the naked and comatose form of one of Victor's girlfriends ("Alice, I'm a *doctor*," he reminds his wife later; she's hardly reassured), Sandor tries to seduce Alice. And even though she breaks away from him to look for her husband, as the orchestra plays "I Only Have Eyes For You," Sandor seems to have impregnated her anyway. She leaves the party bearing an imp who will be born the next night, when, stoned and provoked by Bill's presumptions about her and women in general, and exhausted by what it is he thinks that women really want, she makes her "confession": her story about the stranger, a naval officer she saw only in passing the summer before, and how in one moment she wanted him so completely that she would have been willing to leave her husband and child forever to spend one night with him. And just like that, spontaneously, she gives birth to unwanted, necessary Honesty and its very unpleasant twin, Jealousy. The movie that starts running in Bill's head is the one that everybody wanted to see in the first place.

Revenge fucking may not be the sweetest sex, nor the most satisfying, but it's the most urgent. It's also almost always a wretched futility, and it requires good character and better luck to avoid it. Tied to a whipping post he didn't even know existed before, Dr. Bill goes off on a two-day trajectory through the desire realms without ever knowing what it is that he actually desires. He experiences plenty of sexual abrasions—he's gay-bashed, importuned, receives an unwanted confession of love, and has his life threatened—but never sex. He keeps leaving the dugout but he never steps up to the plate. (One critic called it "a series of erotic misadventures," completely missing the point, and another presumed to know what "the audience" had learned about marriage and sex from the films of the past century, particularly from Bergman, without considering all that this same audience had forgotten in the more than twenty-five years since the movies became balkanized by television.)

Without making ignorant assumptions about the actual sex life of Tom Cruise and Nicole Kidman (the focus of so much speculation in the coverage and even the reviews of *Eyes Wide Shut*), they certainly proved to my satisfaction that they knew how to play a beautiful, happily married couple in love in a movie. No one could have been surprised by Nicole Kidman's acting, but once the reviewers paid tribute to Tom Cruise's status as a major movie star, most went on to dismiss his amazing performance. Like Ryan O'Neal, Jack Nicholson, and Matthew Modine before him, Tom Cruise gave Stanley his money's worth. He created the perfect vehicle to carry one of the film's most original and shocking themes. In ways that Schnitzler never even thought about, *Eyes Wide Shut* challenges the ancient and poisonous canard that the erect male member has no conscience.

Stanley Kubrick and rainbows, Stanley Kubrick and party lights, Stanley Kubrick on behalf of love and marriage, chastity, and the secrets of women; *What on earth is going on here?* For a movie that offers glimpses of a lurid night-time underworld, and which has a powerful current of morbidity running through it, *Eyes Wide Shut* has a remarkably sunny disposition. There's a sweetness to most of the people in the film, and to most of the performances. (It was probably bad for Stanley's misanthropic image to project a hero as decent as Bill Harford.) The colors are exquisite, glowing and pulsing, soothing, like some lavish opium-dream version of *The Nutcracker*, reminiscent of movies like *Fanny and Alexander, Lola Montes, Vertigo, One from the Heart* (which was originally conceived as the first X-rated film to use big stars), and any number of films by Vincente Minnelli or Michael Powell. Those eloquent, discreet fades that Stanley has always been the master of have never been more dramatic. As film, it has all of the qualities that you'd think film critics would look for, pray for, sit through many hours of completely empty viewing hoping to one day enjoy, and it all sailed clean through their nets. All that remained to seal their aversion to *Eyes Wide Shut* was a happy ending, and it also had that: Standing in the middle of a toy store, speaking the verities that are at least as old as marriage and with no guile whatsoever, like characters at the end of a children's play or the closing moments of *The Magic Flute*, having passed through their ordeals successfully, having told each other "everything," they're ready to go home for a heart-to-heart fuck and a refreshment of their vows.

* * *

I know that it's only a movie, and if it's a masterpiece (as I'm sure it is), that's all that it is, another masterpiece. As rare as they are, somehow the world is teeming with them. If the process of making them had somehow stopped a hundred years ago, and there was no Joyce, no Picasso, no Faulkner or Frank Lloyd Wright, Schoenberg or Ellington or Hitchcock, we would still have far more masterpieces than we'd ever have time to deal with. Maybe (and wouldn't it be pretty to think so?) that's what happened with *Eyes Wide Shut* and the critics; maybe they weren't suffering from art-phobia at all, maybe it was only masterpiece fatigue.

In any event, I won't offend their sense of perfection by suggesting, except very quickly, that flaws can make a masterpiece even more lovable. All of Stanley's movies are flawed, along with just about everybody else's. *The Shining* is famously flawed, and I've never had any idea at all what he thought he was doing in the second half of *Full Metal Jacket*, with the mood swings and the flat satirical intrusions, none of which diminishes its greatness. Not only is *Eyes Wide Shut* a flawed masterpiece, like *War and Peace* and Mahler's Eighth (and, come to think of it, *Fidelio*), I believe it's an unfinished masterpiece (like *The Castle*, and the Mozart *Requiem*), no matter what was said at the time of Stanley's death. He would have fiddled and futzed with it right up to the moment of release and beyond, if he thought he could tune it any finer.

Michael Herr

He might, for example, have done something about what I can only call "the repetitive device" in the dialogue, a line from one character repeated by another, usually in the form of a question: "He moved to Chicago." "He moved to Chicago?" "I had you followed." "You had me followed?" "It was fake." "It was fake?" "Yes, fake."—dozens of times, so many of them that you feel the script would have been half as long without them. They're clearly deliberate, but I can't imagine why, unless possibly to suggest the power of sexual confusion, the worst confusion there is, the only exception I can think of being the confusion experienced in dreams. He probably would have trimmed the undeniable *longueurs*, like the scene near the end where Tom Cruise and Sydney Pollack circle a Matisse-red pool table for what feels like an hour and seem to explicate all the things in the "story" that should never be spoken of. I don't know what to think of it; no man could have wished it longer, and though it's an incredibly interesting scene in many ways, I don't even know what it's supposed to be about, unless, as I suspect, it's really about the red pool table. You could always count on Stanley every time to vote for Beauty over Content, since he didn't think of them as two separate things.

Mark Twain called nostalgia "mental and moral masturbation," meaning, I'll guess, the unhealthy, somewhat selfish, totally uncreative uses of the past, the truth of your history cannibalized for the purposes of sentimentality, pissed away for candy. (It's the element that kept the larger wheels of cinema greased for a hundred years; it's the glop that drips from every orifice of the culture, clogging all our arteries of discrimination.) I hope, then, that I won't be thought a nostalgic fool if I insist that even in my lifetime there was a much more attractive culture than the one we're enjoying now.

They speak about the dumbing of America as a foregone thing, already completed, but, duh, it's a process, and we haven't seen anything yet. The contemplation of this culture is not for sissies, and speaking about it without becoming shrill is increasingly difficult, maybe impossible. In spite of this, even for those of us who were most attached to it, there are better things to do than cling to the wreckage of the liberal-humanist literary culture that seemed so invincible and irreproachable only thirty years ago, to forever pick over the debris and salt it with our tears. Nevertheless, I can understand why people miss it. At its most radiant, it didn't just shine its light into literature but suffused all the arts, the movies most of all.

The Art House Transmission that Stanley received so deeply in the forties was still manifesting in the early sixties, when I spent my nights and a lot of afternoons rocketing between the Bleecker Street Cinema, the Thalia, the New Yorker, and the Museum of Modern Art, running after the hundreds of films that had been unavailable to me living upstate, in the provinces. Films by Bergman, Resnais,

Michael Herr

Kurosawa, Ophuls, Satyajit Ray, Antonioni, Visconti, Buñuel, Bresson, Godard, Melville, Fellini, to say nothing of Sirk, Lang, Hitchcock, Nicholas Ray, Sam Fuller, and not forgetting the final films of Ford and Hawks and Renoir, blew in and out of New York with great velocity and frequency. It's amazing how much luster those names had, and for how many people. They kept that arbitrary rectangle brimming with drama and spectacle, nuance and magic. And so if I got weepy when the end credits rolled on *Eyes Wide Shut* and the waltz played one more time, it wasn't because a movie was over, or because it was the final work of a man I admired and loved, but because that tradition, with its innocence, or anyway its naivete, and a purity that only someone born before 1930 could continue, had come to a certain end, as most traditions do. It's gone and it won't be returning.

It's interesting, that a guy who fancied himself the von Clausewitz of movie marketing, who was so immersed in the arcana of demographics, audience profiles, and distribution strategies, right down to the capacity and turnover of dozens, maybe hundreds, of individual movie theaters, was also a man who made his movies totally for himself. He was calculating, but his truest calculations were all artistic ones. The rest, the behavior he was notorious for, was only show-business phenomena. He didn't grumble about the bankruptcy of a world that welcomed and actually required such manipulations, he was amused and instructed by it, and he played the game pretty well, although perhaps not as well as he thought. Still, no artist could help but find it objectionable.

"How can I make a movie that would gross as much as *Star Wars* and yet allow me to retain my reputation for social responsibility?" Stanley said to Brian Aldiss, whose work they were adapting together for *AI*, the "Pinocchio story." I gather Aldiss had his ups and downs with Stanley, but he tells this story with obvious affection, and acknowledges, naturally, that Stanley was joking. As I hear him tell it in my head, I can pick up on that very distant, almost offstage laugh that made you wonder if you were meant to hear it or not, until you remembered who you were talking to. If Stanley didn't want you to hear something, his dogs might pick it up, but not you. I've never said that he wasn't secretive, and I would *never* say that he wasn't obsessive.

You could always tell it was a Stanley Kubrick movie the moment it started, but he never made the same movie twice. It was often said that the people in Stanley's movies live in separate spaces on the screen, most often alone no matter what the company, but that was something that had been in the air since the early days of the late century; we've all breathed it, artists breathed it more deeply, and exhaled it as work. It was through those spaces, and in the distances between them, and their arrangement on the screen, that you can find the essence of Stanley's sympathy, a valuable quality that he had but that not very many people thought that he had, and which was made even more valuable by his detachment. In all of the media's mischief and misapprehension, there was a lingering innuendo that he really only made movies to get himself through a bad case of chronic social anxiety disorder, but in fact he had his friends, many of them, who tell another story. An artist's isolation has nothing to do with physical circumstances anyway, with how publicly or privately he seems to be doing his work. It's more about tempo, intuition, experiment, and the kind of silence you don't come by easily these days, and not at all if you're passive. Out of this situation, the only situation he could tolerate, he made films of an incredible purity.

He was often enough dismissed as an inspired mechanic by people who were unaffected by his work. He knew the mechanics as well as anybody, better than a lot of actual mechanics, but he only bothered to master them because of their value to his purpose, the way that writers try to learn their language in some manner that is functional and more than functional. Diane Johnson has spoken of his "chaste and rigorous view of art," and Garrett Brown, the inventor of the steadicam and Stanley's partner in a technological marriage made in heaven, recalls, "We had discussions about the elusive quality of perfection." I'm absolutely certain that they did. It was Stanley's subject.

Photograph Credits